AD AX

D1335667

To Dinah!

This paperback edition first published in 2015 by Andersen Press Ltd.

First published in USA in 2010 by Clarion Books.

Published in Australia by Random House Australia Pty., Level 3, 100 Pacific Highway, North Sydney, NSW 2060.

Text and Illustration copyright © David Wiesner, 2010.

The rights of David Wiesner to be identified as the author and illustrator of this work have been
asserted by him in accordance with the Copyright, Designs and Patents Act, 1988.

All rights reserved.

Printed and bound in Malaysia by Tien Wah Press.

David Wiesner has used acrylic, pastel, watercolour and India ink in this book.

10   9   8   7   6   5   4   3   2   1

British Library Cataloguing in Publication Data available.

ISBN 978 1 84939 267 9

This book has been printed on acid-free paper

ART & MAX

DAVID WIESNER

ANDERSEN PRESS

The name is Arthur.

I can paint too, Arthur!

You, Max? Don't be ridiculous.

Oh, all right.

Just don't get in the way.

Well…you could paint me.

You? Really?

What are you doing?

I'm painting you!

Ta-da! What do you think?

This is preposterous!

Ooh! Turn around—
I missed a spot.

Wow!

Oh, Max…

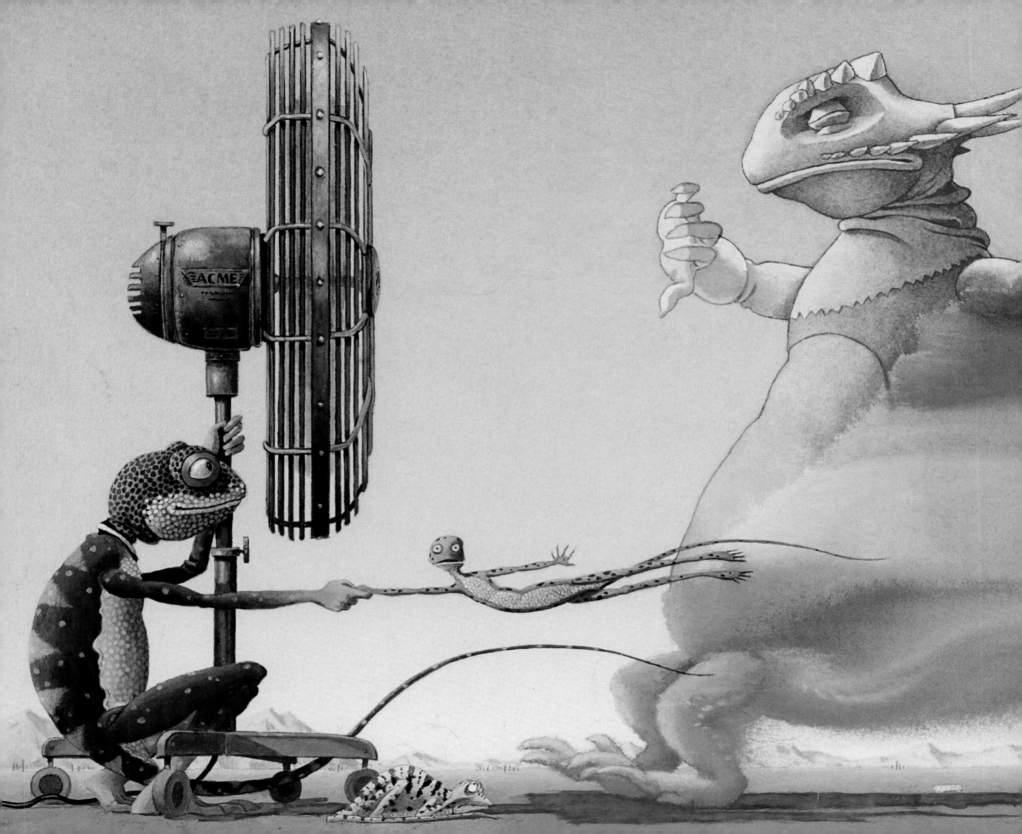

I feel…strange.

Have a drink of water.

I'll get some more!

Oooohhh!

Hold on, Art—

It's *Arthur!*

Don't go...

Arthur?

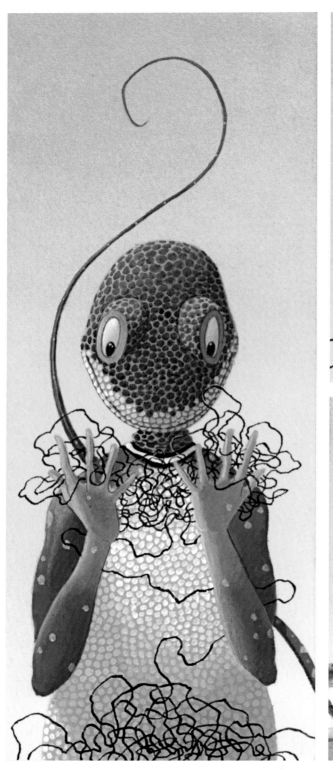

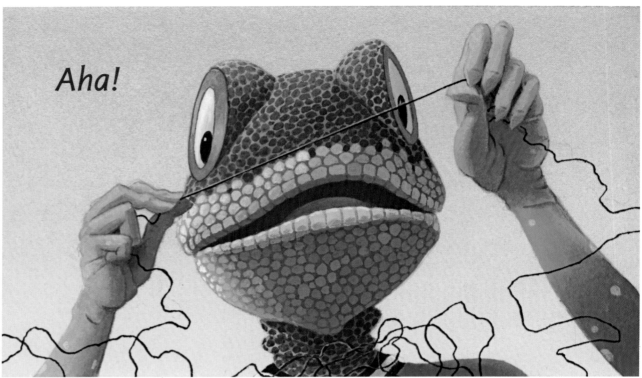

Aha!

OK, here goes!

More detail, I think.

How's that?

Acceptable, I suppose.
But don't forget my foot.

Come back here!
You're not finished!

Now what?

Just hold still, Arthur!

Fascinating.

Yes! Yay!

Let's paint some more!

All right, Max,
let's get started.